MW00880925

JACK'S TALES

BY JIM WESTCOTT
Illustrated by Melissa Fasolino

Copyright © 2015 by Jim Westcott

Illustrations by Melissa Fasolino

Layout & format by Simona Meloni

All rights reserved. This book or any portion thereof may not be
reproduced or used in any manner whatsoever without the express
written permission of the publisher except for
the use of brief quotations in a book review.

Printed in the United States of America by Maple Press.

Distributed by DartFrog, whose titles are exclusive
to independent bookstores.
www.DartFrogDistribution.com

ISBN-10: 0988259966
ISBN-13: 978-0-9882599-6-6

Splashing Cow Books
PO Box 867
Manchester, VT 05254

www.SplashingCowBooks.com

Jack's Tales and being *Jim Westcott the children's author* would merely be bucket list items without the love and support of my wife, Sue. Everything truly meaningful in my life has begun with her. Thank you, Suzy!

CONTENTS

JACK'S
MONSTER

Jack lay in his bed, his eyes closed but his ears open. He was hoping he'd hear rain hammering against his window and a strong wind pushing through the trees outside. Anything to cancel today's fishing trip with his dad. But all he heard were the robins singing their early morning song.

Jack *used* to like fishing with his dad, until his best friend, Brandon, told him what he saw from his cottage dock on Irondequoit Bay - large humps bobbing and sliding in the water near their favorite fishing spot.

Jack opened his eyes to the sunlight on his blanket. His imagination worked overtime. He saw a dragon head, with pointed teeth as long as a ruler, attached to the body of a super-sized snake bobbing and sliding toward Jack's and his dad's boat. Questions and answers filled his mind.

Could a monster really live in Irondequoit Bay?

Sure, and it's probably the Loch Ness Monster's first cousin!

Maybe he's a vegetarian?

With teeth like that? You're crazy.

Jack heard his dad's footsteps, first outside his room, then creeping inside. He faked a few snores but he couldn't fool his dad for long.

"Oh, hey, Dad," Jack said in his best sleeping voice.

"Time to get up, buddy. We need an early start for when they're hungry!"

Hungry? Hungry! Jack hoped his dad was talking about fish, not monsters.

How could he tell his dad he didn't want to go fishing because of what Brandon had seen? His only choice was to stick it out and hope for the best, which meant not becoming breakfast for a prehistoric water monster. And if a Bay Monster *did* eat him, at least it would be quick.

Disappointing his dad could last forever.

By breakfast, with the gruesome thoughts still swirling in his mind, Jack had gloom and doom written on his face. But his dad was too excited to notice. "First time out this season, Jack," Dad said, slurping his coffee. "We're gonna catch us a monster!"

Jack's Froot Loops, which were almost down his throat, quickly made their way back. He slugged his glass of orange juice to stop the coughing. "Sorry, Dad."

"Sure you're okay, son?" He was slapping Jack's back.

Jack swallowed, caught his breath, and wiped his mouth.

"All good, Dad."

"Then off we go! The car's already loaded."

ഇൻ

As his dad drove, eyes straight ahead, Jack watched his favorite sights go by the window. There was the house that looked like a giant capital A. Then the massive corner oak tree he dreamed of climbing one day, if he could muster the courage. There were the stores on Titus Avenue, I-Square, and then Antanolli's Pizza Shop. He smacked his lips, remembering the sweet tomato taste. *Will I ever have the chance to eat a slice again?* he wondered. And then he remembered Brandon's taunts about the Bay Monster eating a Jack Burger. *No more pizza, no more anything after today,* Jack worried.

Once they reached the dock, Jack struggled to focus on fishing. First he left his tackle box in the car. Then he left the bucket of minnows behind. Next he'd forgotten his life jacket. When Jack returned one more time to retrieve his pole, his dad waved his hands in front of his face.

"Earth to Jack!" he joked.

By the time Jack sat quietly at the back of the boat, pole in hand, breathing in the bay water's familiar smell, he couldn't ignore the head-in-the-toilet feeling that had come upon him.

Last chance, Jack! Tell your dad you don't want to go!

Even though he wanted to, he couldn't. How could he explain his fear and the sinking feeling in the pit of his belly?

"You okay, buddy?" Dad asked.

"I'm okay, I think," Jack lied.

"Sure you're ready?"

Jack didn't answer. *Ready to puke,* he was thinking.

The engine rumbled. The water churned from below the motor. Slowly the boat sailed away from the dock.

As they picked up speed, Jack turned toward the shore and watched his safety zone – the dry, safe, monster-free land – disappear. When he finally turned around, he let the cool early morning breeze push past his face and wipe away his tears.

But the Bay Monster remained front and center in his mind. Jack's stomach whirled like a pinwheel. *Don't puke. Don't puke,* he thought, his hands beneath his knees as he stared at the boat's floor.

A passing wave forced Jack to lift his chin. Looking right, he swore in the distance he saw the humped back of a creature cresting the surface, then diving below. Jack's stomach churned until he realized what he saw was nothing more than a chunk of black driftwood. Jack knew driftwood didn't feast on fathers and sons.

The boat soon slowed and glided to a stop. *This is sitting duck position for sure,* Jack realized, looking around. *Or rather, a sitting JACK position.* He filled his lungs with Irondequoit Bay's cool air, trying to tap down his fear. *Maybe if there IS a monster, he'll stay below.*

ℰℛ

"This is it, buddy," Jack's father announced. He stood at the stern, his back to Jack. "My secret sources told me not to tell anyone about this special fishing spot, but I can tell you. Don't say anything to anyone," he added.

Not gonna, Dad, because we're both gonna be monster bait, Jack thought. He was about to tell his dad what Brandon had seen when he noticed his dad's unusually wide smile.

"Jack," he declared, "there's a monster right in this very spot!"

Thanks, Dad! Jack thought. *That's exactly what I wanted to hear.*

Jack's father had already moved into his "lure zone," seated opposite his tackle box so he could examine each and every lure as if for the first time.

Jack quietly gulped and began to lean over. *Don't puke, Jack. Don't puke.*

He could feel his Froot Loops rising up to make an appearance, but then he felt his dad's hand grab the back of his shirt and pull him upright.

"Hey! No goofing around. You might fall in!"

Jack's dad tightened his life jacket. "Earth to Jack!" he blurted, waving his hand in Jack's face. "Remember the knot I taught you how to make? What are you using? A lure or bait?"

Jack's brain suddenly turned on. "I think I'm going to use a minnow."

Jack attached a bright orange bobber to his line about two feet above his hook and swirled his fingers in the bucket until he had one unlucky minnow in the palm of his hand.

"I know how you feel," Jack whispered as he put the hook through the minnow's tail. He cast his line out, watching the bobber follow the minnow as it broke the water's surface. The bobber stilled and Jack's mind sped up, tossing out questions and answers again.

Do sea monsters sleep during the day and hunt at night, like vampires?

You heard Brandon. He saw it in daytime!

Do sea monsters sense fear, like bears and bees do?

If they do, Dad and I are monster bait!

Jack's reel screeched and brought him back to Earth. The sun felt like a dragon's breath on his face. The bay water smelled stronger than ever.

Somehow the bobber had disappeared! His legs trembled. When he was able to steady himself against the side of the boat, he tried to turn his reel but he could barely move the handle.

For an eight-year-old who was almost nine, Jack was awesome at fishing, but suddenly he forgot what to do! Before he knew what was happening, his arms stretched over the side of the boat like they were string cheese. Whatever was on the other end of his line had taken his minnow and his hook and now it wanted his line and his bobber and his pole and maybe even their boat and then Jack and his dad would be next! *I should have told Dad about the monster!* he thought. "MONSTER! MONSTER!" he heard himself yelling.

"Hang on, Jack!" his dad shouted. He'd grabbed Jack's handle and screwed it back into his reel.

Now it was Jack's turn to grab the handle, turning it in the right direction.

"You can do this, Jack!" his dad shouted. "Keep reeling it in!"

Jack used his left hand to grip the pole, holding it tight against his stomach.

Suddenly, whatever was below decided it was done playing. The sudden release in tension caused the pole to nearly jump out of Jack's grip.

"Is the line snagged?" his father asked, holding his hand around the pole.

"I don't know, Dad. It isn't moving. I can't move it!"

"Take your time. Don't force it. This is something big, Jack!"

You have no idea! Jack thought.

Jack's arms were weakening. *I should just let go. Am I loco or what?*

But then the line moved slowly toward the boat and stopped.

"It's no snag," Jack said, watching the line slice through the dark water again, cutting a V-shape toward the bow. Then it stopped. But Jack could still feel weight on the other end - a lot of it. Sweat dripped from his forehead. His breath was forced.

"Play it just right, Jack," his dad whispered, almost as if he was worried that whatever was on the other end of the line would hear their plan.

"If you pull too hard, Jack, you'll lose everything. If you give it too much, it will take everything," his dad said.

Jack wished there was a third option.

His small hand turned the reel, slow at first, but then faster, turning round and round until whatever he'd hooked began swimming toward the boat, not pulling away. It was waiting beneath the boat and Jack could feel its eerie presence. Jack closed his eyes. There was no more line to reel in. It was time to finally meet the monster.

Ωℛ

Cold bay water thrashed over the side of the boat, hitting Jack's arms and face. If he opened his eyes, he might see the monster! But he couldn't resist. Blinking both eyes open, Jack saw, to his horror, his father hanging over the edge of the boat. He was fighting for his life. He was about to be something's breakfast!

It *should have been* the scariest moment of his life. After all, he was about to come face to face with what had been scaring him all morning. But he didn't dissolve into a puddle. He didn't morph into a human ball and hide in the corner. He didn't scream like a baby because someone had stolen his binky. Instead, he got angry! This thing would have to go through him first before he messed with his dad!

"Not today!" he yelled. "You're not messing with me!" Jack wrapped his arms around his father's waist. "I'm not letting you go, Dad!"

But just then his dad swung around, the fish net secured firmly in his hands. And when he released it, something landed on the boat's floor with a THUD!

OH, NO! Jack thought. *The beast was in the boat!*

There were more thuds until something slimy, wet, and cold slapped Jack's ankle.

"It's a monster!" Jack's dad screamed. "I don't believe it!"

Jack grabbed a wooden oar and readied to pummel the beast. "Leave us alone!" he roared.

"Die, you monster!"

Jack's dad grabbed the oar, pulled it loose from Jack's hands and chest-hugged his son.

"You did it! You did it!"

What? Jack wondered. *What was his dad talking about?*

"You just caught the biggest monster I've ever seen, Jack!"

Jack gawked at the net. The sneering fish was spiked, with black spots down its side. Its slimy tail and flippers took Jack's breath away.

"It's bigger than any pike I've ever caught, son. At least fifteen pounds!" He'd crouched to the floor so his eyes were even with Jack's.

Jack felt his heartbeat slow. The word "pike" kept repeating in his head. *Pike! Fish! Monster? No. Just a fish.*

His arms and legs went limp like spaghetti. *What a beautiful catch!*

Jack studied the pike, noting its white stomach, its glistening scales, and the bright pink color inside its gills.

Jack and his dad studied its teeth, ran their fingers down its side, and checked its fins.

"It's calm now, Jack, and tired. He can't harm us."

Just a few minutes earlier it had been the horrific Bay Monster. But now?

"What should we do with it, Dad?" Jack asked.

But he knew the answer the minute he'd asked the question.

"We should put it back in the water, Dad."

"You sure, buddy? This is the kind that gets mounted on walls."

"It needs to go back, Dad. Seeing it on a wall would just make me sad."

Before they returned their catch to the water, Jack's dad steadied the gigantic pike in Jack's hands. "Careful now. You got it?" Jack nodded as his dad positioned the camera and took a picture.

Once they returned the fish to the water, Jack savored every moment - the sun on his face, the slap of the wind, the strong smell of the bay, and the ride back home.

Best of all, he realized Brandon had been right. There really *was* a monster in Irondequoit Bay.

But unlike Brandon, Jack had proof.

JACK'S PIZZA GHOST

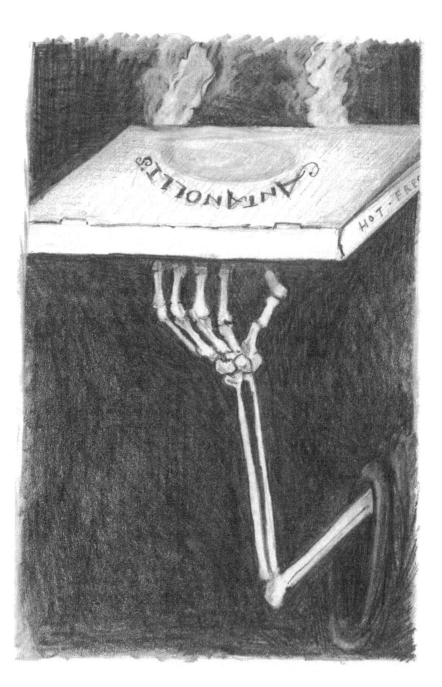

Jack liked to call what happened the Parking Lot Incident. Every time he thought about it, he could feel himself breathe easier. At least sort of.

It was October and soccer season, just four months after he'd caught that monster fish with his dad. And there he was again, this time at his brother Andrew's soccer game, worried and afraid. He'd run back to their car to retrieve his dad's wallet, but when he returned, his dad was nowhere to be found.

The late afternoon sun scorched his face, even though the day was crisp. He felt his legs wobble and his mind whirl. He plopped his shaky body down on to the sidewalk. He was having another full-blown panic attack, and believe it or not, he swore the attack had sat down next to him. Jack was on a mountain ledge – at least that's what it felt like – and he was falling, falling, falling, with nothing below to catch him. And then he heard his dad's voice.

"Hey, Jack?"

When Jack lifted his head, his dad, who had come looking for him, saw something wasn't right. Jack's tears were the give-away.

"Where'd you go, Dad?" Jack shouted. "You left me! You were gone!"

"I was just to the side of the stands, buddy, talking to Jared's dad. I thought you saw me."

Jack's dad hugged him. "What's going on, son?"

So much for keeping this inside me, Jack thought. Then and there he 'fessed up to his panic attacks, including last summer's when they'd caught that monster pike. Deep down he'd always thought his dad knew about them anyway.

Jack's dad pulled him even closer and, just like that, Jack's mountain ledge evaporated. But as

Jack hugged his father, he knew there were other fears on the horizon, like the ghost in their basement, which his brother Andrew had challenged him to confront.

ഈരു

It was now or never, the boys knew, once Jack's mom and dad left for the afternoon.

Andrew had promised Jack and Brandon memberships in his Irondequoit Paranormal Club, if they could rid the basement of the ghostly presence.

"Check the knot again," Jack ordered his best friend since kindergarten, who had tied a rope to Jack's waist, so he could haul him back if the ghost decided to snatch Jack up. "Make it tight, but not *too* tight. I need to breathe."

Jack was down on one knee, unzipping the backpack they'd prepared.

One iPod with video and audio. *Check.*

One flashlight. *Check.*

One boxed, microwaved pepperoni and sausage pizza, still kind of warm. *Check.*

"Hey, wait a minute!" Jack said, looking inside the box. "There were six slices to begin with. Now there are four!"

"You don't really think ghosts can eat, do you?" Brandon asked. "Even if they could swallow, where would it go?"

Tomato sauce covered Brandon's mouth. It wasn't Antanolli's pizza, but Jack figured the ghost wouldn't care. *There's no such thing as bad pizza,* he told himself. *I hope that's true for ghosts too.*

Brandon pulled the rope tighter. "Ready, Jack?"

"If something grabs me, you can't let it take me, man!"

Brandon wiped his mouth. "Never!"

Originally, Jack had thought Brandon would go along with him, but then he changed his mind. Brandon would likely call out the ghost for not going to heaven, which would be offensive. Even if the ghost *used* to live in their house, Jack knew from watching his ghost-hunting TV shows that it wouldn't be a good idea to tick him off.

Jack turned to test the rope and noticed Brandon's mouth was all scrunched-up.

"You know, you don't *have* to go in there...." Brandon said nervously.

"I guess I want to know," Jack said.

"Know what?"

"If there are...you know....when we...." Jack stammered.

"When we what?" Brandon asked.

Jack waved him off. "Never mind, man. Nothing."

Except it wasn't nothing. In fact, it was a lot of *somethings* because that's how it always went with Jack and his worrying. The panic attacks had become less frequent, but not the worries. Jack worried about everything.

Why did he want to join Andrew's stupid club anyway?

Who WAS this ghost, and why WASN'T it in heaven?

And now his parents were forty-something and what if they didn't live past fifty and where would they be if they weren't here anymore?

For just a second, Jack thought of sharing his worries with Brandon. But maybe that was a conversation way outside what two guys, best friends or not, could handle?

The worries multiplied, bouncing around like atoms in a microwave nuking pizza.

If he didn't soon distract himself, *that scary feel-*

ing would return, the one he felt for the first time when he was six and lost track of his mom in the Eastonview Mall. By the time the security guards brought him to their office, he was sure he'd grow up to be a homeless mall orphan!

I'm doing it again, Jack thought. But that's when he made up his mind to confront the basement ghost. Somehow he knew, deep inside, that the only way to move past his panic attacks would be to muster the courage to confront his fears.

Jack's trembling hand turned the basement door's knob. The worn, dark door was better suited for a tomb. He yanked at the rope around his waist, gave Brandon a thumbs up and opened the door.

Jack stared in silence at the blackness that greeted him.

ℰᏩ

As he stepped down the staircase into the dark, clutching the pizza box in his fists, the musty smell invaded his nose.

I'm a whack job! Jack told himself. He could hear his heart knocking.

Whack job! Whack job!

But I HAVE pizza!

Maybe the ghost misses pizza?

He'll like me if I give him some!

But what if he DOESN'T like pizza?

Jack jerked his head about, trying to rid his brain of the demon image.

"Are you okay, man?" Brandon called down from the top of the stairs.

"I'm good," Jack hollered, steadying his voice.

Turning on his pocket flashlight helped. He saw

old paint cans against one wall and the furnace against another. A dark sheet covered what must have been boxes stacked in front of the furnace. Jack shone the flashlight into all four corners. Nothing unusual popped up.

There! Jack thought. *I faced my fear so now it's time to go!*

But that's when Jack saw a very strange shape across the room.

What the…?

The longer Jack stared, the longer he worried. It wasn't moving, but it was a creepy looking shape. Not human, for sure.

Wait a minute. Is that Dad's crazy wild-west camera? The one with three legs that looks like an insect born inside a nuclear waste dumping ground! Jack could feel his stomach muscles loosen.

Phew! Just a dirty basement with dad's freakazoid camera! Jack exhaled.

He'd almost calmed down completely when the scratching noise began. It was the sound of fingernails sliding across metal.

Jack's legs froze. Remembering the pizza plan, his hands lifted the box and opened the lid. From somewhere and something came...

"*FROOOOOOOOZZZZEN...PIIIIIIIZZZZZ-ZAAAAAA?*"

Why Jack didn't Frisbee-toss the box into the darkness and run back up the stairs, he didn't have a clue. Why be began talking to whatever was there with him was even more mysterious.

"I-I-I'm s-s-sorry," he whispered before taking a deep breath. "I didn't have enough money for real pizza, like from Antanolli's. And even if I did," he continued, "I can't drive because I'm only nine and I don't have a license."

Jack reached into the box and removed a slice.

"This isn't that bad, though. Even bad pizza's good, right? Take a slice!"

But nothing happened.

"You can have all four!" Jack offered.

Again, nothing.

The ghost wasn't answering *or* eating, that much was clear to Jack. He stepped toward the stairs to leave, which is when he was blinded by flashes of white light!

"Get me outta here, Brandon!" Jack yelled, instinctively covering his eyes amidst the erupting bursts of light.

Jack was frantically making his way up the stairs, with Brandon pulling hard, when he tripped on the rope and fell.

Any minute now the ghost would be standing over him, trapping him in the darkness.

"Goodbye, Mom and Dad!" Jack whispered.

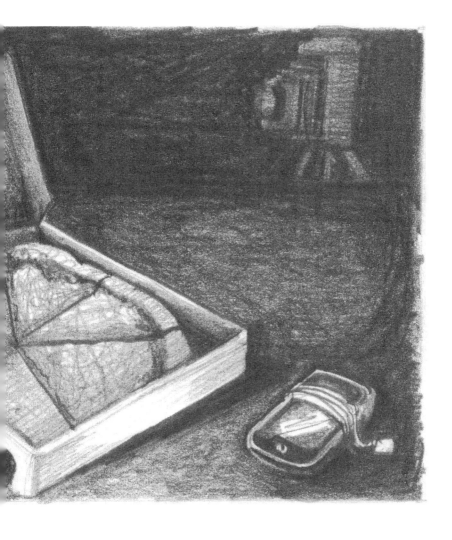

"Goodbye, Andrew! Goodbye, Brandon!"

Jack felt a sharp pain around his waist. Then he felt another.

"I don't wanna die," Jack yelled out.

"Get up," Brandon yelled from the top of the stairs. That's when Jack realized that the pains he felt around his waist were from Brandon's aggressive tugs on the rope, not from the ghost. The third tug was the hardest, forcing Jack back on to his feet. He bolted up the stairs and through the door.

Brandon tried to slam the door shut behind Jack, but something got in the way. It was a foot.

Before Jack and Brandon could ready their punches (which really wouldn't do much to a ghost, anyway), Andrew leapt through the door and grabbed Brandon by the shoulders, hooking him beneath his arms and swinging him around in laughter.

Soon Brandon's brother Sean had Jack in the same hold.

"YOU TWO BETTER RUN!" they shouted. "THE GHOST IS GONNA GET YOU!"

"YEAH! WE WANT ANTANOLLI'S, NOT FROZEN!" their friend Jared yelled, the last to arrive.

He tussled Jack's hair. "Sorry, little guy. But it was your brother Andrew's idea. Pretty great prank, huh!"

"Yeah," Andrew said, punching Jack's arm. "That camera of Dad's really works; cord, flash, and all. We were behind the boxes the whole time. Gotcha bro!"

Jack's eyes were already red and watery. "You're a jerk, Andrew! And so are your two IPC members!"

"Yeah, jerk, jerk, and jerk!" Brandon called after them, as the three ran off laughing.

Brandon put his hand on Jack's shoulder and

tried to smile. "At least they weren't ghosts."

"Total jerks," Jack repeated.

"Can I tell you something?" Brandon asked.

"What?" Jack whispered, still visibly shaken by the ambush.

"I was too scared to go down there," Brandon said, as he looked toward the basement stairs. "I wish I had courage like you."

This time Jack tried to smile.

"Hey, look!" Jack said, pointing to the four pizza slices that had fallen to the floor.

"Two-Minute Rule still stands, right?"

Jack smiled a full smile now. "Always."

இஅ

Jack had been quietly standing outside Andrew's bedroom for what seemed like hours, peeking through the half-opened door. Andrew, Sean, and Jared were zoned out on their laptop screens, ear buds in.

Their conversation had Jack grinning.

"What we did to your brother was pretty mean," Sean said.

"Yeah, but he took it a whole lot better than you said he would," Jared answered.

Andrew agreed, laughing. "I thought he'd never it make it down the stairs!"

Once the three were lost in their screens again, Jack tip-toed through the door, snuck up behind his brother and tapped him on the head. Andrew sprung up like a ready Pop Tart, ripping out his ear buds.

"What the —?" Andrew bellowed.

"Gotcha," Jack blurted, as he pulled his iPod from his cargo pants pocket. "Wanna see what a *real* ghost looks like?"

Andrew pushed his little brother, ordering him out of his room, but Jack was staying. "I've got something on my iPod you might want to see," Jack said, as he dug his feet into the carpet and shoved the iPod in Andrew's face.

"Do you see it?"

"See what?" Andrew barked, as he stared at the dark screen.

"What is it?" Sean asked.

"There! Right there!" Jack said, pointing to something black moving across the screen.

Jack watched their faces turn white as a voice came through the iPod speaker.

"*Andrewwwww, Antinool, Andrewwww, Antinool, Andrewwww....*"

"Who's that talking?" asked Jared.

Jack shrugged his shoulders. "I don't know whose speaking. I didn't hear anything when I was recording down in the basement except for the stuff you guys said."

The three IPC members looked dumbfounded.

"All I know is that it's not me. Maybe your hoax ticked off a real ghost?" Jack shook his head, then eyeballed his brother. "And it seems to be fixed on *you*, Andrew."

Suddenly everyone had someplace else to be. Sean at home. Jared at practice.

Jack tapped Andrew's shoulder again. "Sounds to me like it wants pizza," Jack said, as he headed out the door and down the hall toward his bedroom. "And sounds like he wants it from you."

ಐಂಬ

When Brandon stopped by the next day, he found Jack in the basement.

"Pizza!" Brandon said. "I smell Antanolli's pizza!" He descended the stairs easily, something he had been unwilling to do the day before. When he reached the bottom step, he found Jack sitting at a table set for two, with an Antanolli's pizza in the middle.

"Have a seat, my friend," Jack said.

"How did…" Brandon began to ask in a confused tone. "Your mom and dad, right?

"Nope," Jack said.

"Then how'd you get the fifteen bucks to buy a pizza?

"Well, it wasn't me," Jack answered, "and it wasn't the ghost."

Brandon's eyes flashed. "No way! Your brother?"

Jack smiled. "He didn't buy it for *us*. He bought it for the ghost. The pizza ghost!"

Brandon scratched his head. "A pizza ghost?"

Jack took his iPod from his pocket and clicked on the video.

"*Andrewwwww, Antinoool...*"

Jack could hardly contain himself, showing his friend how he'd put a shadow ghost in the video and used an app to download the creepy voice.

"Andrew personally delivered the pizza, and then ran back up stairs. I've never seen him run faster! I think he's at soccer practice now."

"Serves him right," Brandon laughed, before chomping on the slice Jack had just served him.

Jack took a mammoth bite of his slice. "Guess who's now in the IPC too?" He asked.

Brandon looked stunned. "You're kidding me, right?"

Jack stopped chewing. "But I don't want to be in the club anymore."

"We can just start our own club, Jack."

They both took a few more bites of the pizza, nodding in agreement at the thought of their own club.

Brandon broke the silence after swallowing a bite too big for most mouths to handle. "Hey Jack, do you worry about what it's really like? You know, not being here some day?" Brandon pointed to the ceiling.

Jack couldn't believe his ears. *Brandon thinks about these things too?*

"Sometimes." He couldn't lie to his best friend.

"That makes two of us," Brandon said. "Do you think others worry about dying too?"

"Maybe everybody does," Jack said matter of factly, as he picked up another piece of pizza. "But I've never asked anyone, to be honest."

Brandon nodded in agreement, before changing the subject. "Maybe Andrew should bring the pizza ghost an Antanolli's every Friday?"

"I couldn't be that mean, not even to Andrew."

Brandon smiled, pulling another slice from the box. "The pizza ghost. That's so awesome."

Jack grinned as he felt a rush of joy flood his insides. His fears were only as real as the pizza ghost, and now he knew it.

JACK'S SAVE

It was *supposed* to be their year, the year the Tornadoes won everything – every soccer game, every play-off, and the U10 Elite Championship title.

Jack believed it more than anyone. He was the goalie, the Stopper. And not just *any* Stopper. He had won fourteen games as the goalie for the Tornadoes, and lost only one.

"Jack will save us!" his teammates shouted. "Jack saves everything!"

That is, until Chris Kirkenburg stole the ball with 80 seconds left in the semi-final game, and passed it to the Cyclones' best scorer, Jeff Thompson.

Jack waited for the sign, the tell, to see where Jeff's eyes looked, how he turned his head, how he shifted his shoulder.

In the one game the Tornadoes *had* lost, which

had been against the Cyclones, Jack had turned away, missing Jeff's tell.

But not this time, Jack told himself.

He was waiting, hands out, feet apart, equal space between the pipes.

I got this. I got this.

But Jeff trapped the ball beneath a cleat, stopped as if he hadn't been sprinting full speed and gently sent the ball into the far left corner of the net.

Jack stood motionless.

The Scorer had scored...again.

The Cyclones were going to the championship game for the second year in a row.

There was the usual pandemonium. Sprints. Howls. Bear hugs. A mound of orange-and-black Cyclone jerseys, shorts, socks, cleats writhing on the field.

The Tornadoes had scattered. Some planted their faces in the grass or rolled on their backs in disbelief. Others left the field to their sideline and parents. A few hung around, to see what this kind of victory looked like.

Jack's coach argued, but lost his case. Jeff's goal hadn't been offsides.

Jack was lost in the loss. Zombie-like, he stood there, waiting for and hoping the ground would open up and swallow him. But when that didn't happen, he dragged himself to the sideline, his cleats digging into the field with each step.

Just before he reached the crowd of onlookers, Jack's mom stepped into his path to hug him.

It was the first s*ad hug* she'd given him in maybe three years, when he was almost seven.

"Great game, Jack," his dad said, rubbing his son's head. His dad and brother Andrew had been right behind his mom. "You did awesome out there. Don't let it get to you, son. You had an amazing season."

Jack felt the squishing of what could only be tears on his mom's shoulder. For a second that scary dark feeling came back, hitting him full force, diving and bombing, searching for an opening. But then it suddenly gave up. Jack took a deep breath, uncoupled from his mom and packed his things on the sideline. He was all-frowns.

‰K

The next day at school, Jack was surprised when lockers didn't slam, talking didn't stop, and nobody turned and stared.

Maybe it won't be so bad, Jack thought.

And then he heard the shouts of "CYCLONES! CYCLONES! CYCLONES!"

It was Xavier, five lockers down, in the middle of a bunch of Cyclones. Jack had forgotten all about Xavier.

He was already thinking up a reason for the school nurse to call his mom when his best friend Brandon appeared out of nowhere.

"Hey! Can I shake the hand of the best soccer goalie ever?" Brandon asked, pumping Jack's hand. "You the man!"

Brandon, it seems, needed Jack's opinion, because he quickly moved on to a different topic. "On a scale of one to ten, ten being the fiercest, how do you think I'd look with a mohawk? A tall, spikey one, like two feet tall. The lacrosse team says I should get one. Maybe I'll make it bright red with black streaks. You know, my team's colors."

Jack swirled a finger in circles near his head.

"You're loco, B."

Brandon had never been afraid of anything, except ghosts maybe, which was totally understandable. Jack loved that about his friend.

"And you can get one too, Jack, only make it Tornado colors – dark green and black. You'd look so nasty, nobody would dare to shoot."

"Yeah, real nasty." Jack motioned with his thumb to the nearby Cyclones. Xavier's voice couldn't be ignored. He was boasting again about yesterday's game.

"You know what, Jack?" Brandon added. "You don't need a mohawk. You're already nasty."

"Yeah, B," Jack said, slamming his locker. "Sure. Whatever."

ဢၐ

Ever since Jack denied every one of Xavier's shots in a soccer game over the summer, Xavier had his heart set on humiliating the Tornadoes' Stopper. And the minute Mrs. Bartell left their classroom to help Madison with her locker, Xavier stood on his chair and continued the taunting.

"Listen up!" He hollered. "Raise your hand if you think the Tornadoes should get a new goalie! Oh, wait! They don't need one anymore. They already lost!"

"Go Z-Man!" Xavier's Cyclone teammates shouted. "Go Z-Man!"

"Hey, See-Man, I didn't get to vote," Brandon said.

"It's Z-Man," Xavier corrected angrily.

"Oh, I'm sorry," Brandon said. "I thought it was See-Man, as in 'See, I thought I was good until Jack rejected me, man!'"

Just like that, Xavier turned into an orangutan, grunting and pounding his chest, daring Brandon to take it outside.

To Jack's surprise, Jeff, the one who had scored the game-winning goal for the Cyclones, ordered Xavier to knock it off and sit down.

Even more surprising was how Xavier dropped his head in embarrassment once he took his seat. Jeff's sportsmanship impressed Jack, who looked back at Xavier with a satisfied glare. But Xavier continued to taunt Jack silently, even after Mrs. Bartell returned. When class was finally over, Jack had had about all he could take of Xavier.

৪০০৪

Jack's video game goalkeeping on the Wii wasn't making him any happier. After school, he had retreated to the family den to play his favorite game. His brother joined in soon thereafter, and sliced a kick past him into the goal, securing a win for his favorite team, Manchester United. The faceless crowd cheered as Jack launched the controller across the room. It skipped off the carpet, hitting Andrew's foot before ricocheting into the wall.

"You're gonna break it, Jack," Andrew said in a scolding tone of voice. "You gotta watch their feet," he said, pointing to the screen. "Don't watch their eyes. Watch their feet."

"I know how to play," Jack said. "I'm better than you."

"No, you're not," Andrew replied, as he began

to move his player around the screen again.

But Jack wasn't interested in watching or even playing now. He was thinking about how nice it would be to become a hermit, right there in his very own den. His mom could slide Antanolli's pizza through a slot in the door and his dad could build him a bathroom. Nobody would bother him. Paradise!

Andrew tossed Jack his controller. "Let me school you again."

School ME? "Prepare to be denied!" Jack grunted.

But when another Manchester United player launched a shot and Jack moved left when he should have moved right, he tossed the controller again. This time when it hit the wall, the back cover came off, sending the batteries flying.

Jack threw himself deep into the couch, burying his face in a pillow. *Hermit Jack* never sounded better.

"Meet me out back at the goal," Andrew said.

Jack heard Andrew digging through the shoe pile in the hallway, then heard the click of his cleats on the mud room floor before the backdoor opened and slammed shut.

ഇൗരു

Jack kicked at the patch of loosened dirt. All he could see was the last second of yesterday's game and Jeff charging at him, about to score.

"Come on," Andrew called, waving Jack into the goal. "Just a few."

They'd been practicing every day after school for over a year. At first, Andrew showed no mercy and Jack hated that. Shots hit him in the face, stung his hands, his arms, his legs. But one day, miserable and battered, Jack dove at a shot to the back left corner, a shot that had gone in a bazillion times before. But this time Jack saved it, sending him home that night with a purpose.

"Ready?" Andrew asked.

Jack stood there, his hands in his pockets, rigid as a pole, tasting the pizza he'd had for lunch in the aroma of his silent burp.

"Earth to Jack!" Andrew called, sounding like their dad.

"Chill man," Jack barked, as he bent down and slapped his thighs. But when Andrew finally kicked the ball, Jack didn't flinch. He just stood there, staring at Andrew, as the ball streaked by his face.

"Are you trying to be brave or are you just stupid?" Andrew asked.

Jack struck a pose and smiled. "I'm practicing for my new job as an artist's model."

Ignoring his brother's antics, Andrew dribbled to Jack's right, turned in a half circle, picked up speed, faked left, cut right, and shot. "SCORE!"

Jack stopped posing, grabbed the ball from underneath the net and threw it as hard as he could at Andrew's face.

Andrew caught the ball before it hit him. "Don't be mad, man."

"I'm not," Jack said, starting for the house.

"Where you going?"

"I'm done!" Jack said.

"Hey!" Andrew called. "Any chance you want to know WHY Jeff scored on you yesterday?"

The words stopped Jack. He knew why. At least, he *thought* he knew why.

"Because I stink!" he shouted, turning to face his

brother. "In case you forgot, we were supposed to win the championship!"

No matter what Andrew said, how he'd failed lots of times himself, how he knew how Jack felt, how he knew Jack was a fighter – none of it could change Jack's mind.

"Then let me have one more shot at you. I promise NOT to feel sorry for you."

That one little word, "sorry," stopped Jack in his tracks and turned him around.

"Sorry, huh?" Jack said, once he was back in the net. He lowered his body, hands out, knees bent, feet wide as he swiped at the line in front of him.

"Jack, look at me," Andrew ordered. His voice sounded different. "Just to make this fair,"

he said, "watch my legs, watch my feet, okay. The legs always tell you where the ball is going!"

Then he came at the net, dribbling slowly to the

right, circling back, moving to the right, to the left, taking his time until he picked up speed, cut fast to his right, and rocketed one.

The ball hit Jack's raised hands before it found its new path, heading straight for their dad's car, bouncing off the windshield. THUNK!

"See, you're full of it!" Jack shrieked. "Full, full, full." He turned and shook his butt at Andrew.

"Just so you know," Andrew admitted, "there was a time *I* didn't want to play anymore. But Dad told me to stick it out, and I'm glad I did." Before Jack knew it, Andrew had him in a hold and was knuckling his head like one of the Three Stooges. "For what it's worth, I'm proud of you, Jack."

Jack waited for the insult that always followed – something like, "…even though you're the most annoying turd on the planet."

But it never arrived.

And even if it had, Jack would have soon forgotten it, because of what he heard their mom say as she ran toward them.

Coach had phoned. The Tsunamis had been forced to forfeit. Three players were over-age. The Tornadoes were going to play for the championship after all!

Maybe, Jack thought as adrenaline pumped through his veins, *this COULD BE the year?*

ဆဥ

Jack couldn't wait for Saturday to come.

He'd had a week of rematch talk at school. Jack vs. Jeff. The Scorer vs. The Stopper.

It didn't help when a few of his Tsunami friends – like Daniel and Colin - didn't stick up for him when the other Tsunamis accused him of blowin' it last week.

For his part, Jack just tried to stay focused on Saturday.

But as the game day arrived, the warm-ups were tough. Worries whirled inside Jack's mind.

What if we lose again?

What if I blow it again?

What if everyone's right and I don't deserve to be here?

As both teams took the field. Jack jogged to his goal. The Scorer, Jeff Thompson, stood at mid-field. The Cyclone's center forward kicked the ball into play.

The Tornadoes fought hard but the Cyclones had twice as many shots on goal, their forwards faster than ever. Though Jack had never allowed more than one goal in a game, the Cyclones had already scored three. When Xavier scored the third goal, he ran around the field twirling like an airplane, trying his best to make Jack feel awful.

On the sideline before the fourth quarter began, Jack read his teammates' faces. *They'd already lost. The game was over.* Coach Wilson's face dripped with disappointment.

It's MY fault we're losing, Jack wanted to shout.

The torture continued as Xavier broke away and dribbled, weaving in and out of the Tornado defense, looking way better than he really was. Jack stayed back as Xavier reached the box, sprinted forward and hammered the ball, which headed straight for Jack's face, hitting him flush on the nose. Jack's head jerked with the impact, as the toe of Xavier's right cleat jabbed into Jack's leg. Jack lay on his back in the box, as a Tornado defender kicked the loose ball out of bounds before it went into the net.

Jack's world was blurry at first. But after a few minutes, he sat up with the help of Coach Wilson and his dad. They steadied him, and once he stood, they began walking him to the sidelines.

"I'm good!" Jack insisted suddenly, wrestling his arms away from his dad and Coach Wilson. "I'm playing!" He jogged back toward the net and set himself up in the goalie box. At the goal line, he lowered himself into his denial stance, swiping at the line that decides who wins or loses. Stepping high, he worked off his leg pain.

The cheers Jack heard steeled him. Again he swiped the goal line.

The Tornadoes turned to their opponent's goal. The referee's whistle re-started the game, and it soon became clear that the tide had somehow turned. The Tornadoes scored, then scored again six minutes later, and with two minutes left they tied the game!

Now it was the Tornadoes who were marching down the field, making crisp passes and on target shots. But when Chris Kirkenburg stole the ball and moved it into Tornado-land, pushing past two midfielders before sending it to Jeff Thompson, Jack knew it was déjà vu.

Every hair on his body screamed, *it's happening again!*

The moment the ball touched the Scorer's feet, the crowd on both sides of the field erupted. Jeff weaved to the center of the pitch, streaking, using the seams. Gliding by the last Tornado defender, Jeff now stood twenty-five feet from Jack, which is when Andrew's words screamed in Jack's head.

Watch my legs! Watch my feet! The legs always tell you where the ball is going!"

Jack looked down and followed Jeff's legs. They cut to the left, stopped, and turned right.

When he cocked back his left foot and fired forward, Jack leapt for his life. His chin scraped the ground the exact moment the black-and-white streak stung his fingertips.

The ball found a new path to the Tornado sideline, and then was booted to midfield by a Tornado defender, which is when the ref blew the whistle.

The Stopper had stopped the Scorer, and now the game was over. The U10 Elite Championship game had ended in a tie.

Or had it?

ഏ൚

There was no cheering, no running onto the field, no jumping on anyone.

Just silence…

…until…

the two coaches met with the referee. For the first time ever in U10 Elite history, each team was allowed three penalty kicks.

The Tornadoes would get the first shot. Six shots total, three for each team, twenty feet away from the goalie. Whichever team had the most goals would decide the championship.

Connor went first, lining himself behind the ball, taking two steps, staring hard, then kicking the ball. Tim Crowles, the goalie for the Cyclones, leapt, but in the wrong direction. One point for the Tornadoes!

Next came Michael Kent. Jack was sure he had it! The ball hit him hard as he jumped for it, bending his fingers almost to the breaking point. But the ball glanced off the right post and just made it into the net. Jack got to his feet and spit out dirt. One point for the Cyclones.

Now it was Tyler's turn, who quickly kicked his shot into the far left corner. The Tornado crowd went wild. Add one more point.

This time it was Jack against Chris Kirkenburg. His shot slapped off of Jack's legs as he dove to the left, deflecting it away from the goal. The Tornado fans roared.

When Jerry lined up, all the Tornado fans understood that if he scored, his goal would win the game, putting the Cyclones two goals behind with only one shooter left. But his ball sailed over the top bar and bounced to the parking lot. Cyclone fans sighed in relief, then started cheering for their final shooter. "JEFF! JEFF! JEFF! YOU CAN DO IT, JEFF!"

One more time Jack stood face to face with the Scorer. But this time, he didn't see a confident player. He saw a tired kid about to snap. Jeff's legs were trembling and his hands were shaking. Jack could see him taking deep breaths from where he stood in the goalie box. As Jack looked at Jeff, he realized that he saw a piece of himself. He remembered all the times he'd let that scary feeling get the best of him. When he was six, lost in the mall and couldn't find his mom. When he was scared some monster fish would use his dad and him as bait. When a ghost in the basement had him scared out of his wits. Now that scary feeling had found another kid to pick on, and Jack felt sorry for Jeff.

Jeff was *supposed* to make the shot. After all, he was the Scorer. Jack could almost see those worries whirling through Jeff's mind, almost see the fears that had worked their way inside.

But the time to shoot was upon him, and Jeff lined up his shot. The crowd went wild.

Jack bent his knees, in position, equal space between the pipes. He swiped the line that decides who wins or loses, then scowled at Jeff who quickly scowled back.

The crowd erupted as Jeff's shot lifted off and curved toward the left corner of the net. Jack dove and the ball slammed off his left shoulder, flinging its way into the left side of the net.

Cyclones fans roared, but only for a moment. The realization that there were no more shooters soon cast a hush over the crowd. Both teams had scored two overtime goals.

Jack got up, dirt on his chin, and started walking toward Jeff. He knew just what to do. When he reached the Shooter, he grabbed his limp hand and held it high. As loud as he could, Jack yelled, "This game is a tie!"

It's hard to say who started the stampede, once both teams realized everyone had won. They tackled Jack and Jeff, who soon found themselves on the bottom of an elated dog pile. As the mound of celebratory boys slowly receded, Jack noticed his brother standing on the field.

"Nice job today, champ!" Andrew said. "You saved the game!"

ABOUT JIM WESTCOTT

For nineteen years, my dad taught children and adults who have learning disabilities. He has a master's degree in special education. We live in Irondequoit, New York, and fish all the time in Irondequoit Bay. I really don't get scared like the Jack in this book, but that doesn't mean I don't get freaked out from time to time. There really isn't a ghost in our basement, at least I don't think so. I do play soccer (I'm a forward, but this year I started playing goalie!), and I do have a great friend named Brandon. And oh, Andrew really isn't such a bad brother…well, most of the time. Sorry Dad, is this too much about me?

-Jack

With Dad when I was 8

Other Splashing Cow Books
You May Enjoy

The Mailbox Adventures

Treasure from Lake Titicaca

Tempest over Tahiti

65 Degrees North

The Blue Marble Diaries

This New World

Visit our website for more information

www.SplashingCowBooks.com